DAYS THAT NEVER WERE

JAMES YOUNG

Copyright

Copyright © 2025 by James Young. James Young holds all copyrights to these photos.
All rights reserved.
No portion of this book may be reproduced in any form without written permission from the author. There is absolutely no permission to scan, upload, or otherwise electronically distribute this book for any purpose without written, explicit permission from the author except as permitted by U.S. copyright law. Any use of the images or text by artificial intelligence (AI) is not granted nor will it be granted by the copyright owner. Use of images in this book for AI does not constitute fair use. Author reserves the right to seek legal action against any individual or corporation involved in the reproduction of these images by entities intending to use in conjunction with AI.

Introduction
(a.k.a., "Why is Someone Challenged by Stick Figures Publishing an Art Book?")

I'm certain many of my long-term fans will side eye this project. As this introduction's subtitle indicates, I have regularly proclaimed my negligible artistic abilities. Need a sector sketch with target reference points, battle positions, and fields of fire? Now that I can do, and I promise all who see it will know *exactly* where the bad guys need to die. Want a complex painting of U.S. fast battleships exiting a rain squall to engage the Japanese Center Force? Well, were I to attempt such a project, the hideous end result would cause viewers to apply to the Oedipal School of Optical Solutions lest they behold such terrors again.

So, no, this book is most definitely *not* a surprise reveal of my long-hidden ability / artist's pseudonym. Instead, it's the manifestation of a lifetime love of military art. As a kid, I was a regular reader of the various *Time - Life* historical series. Covering everything from naval warfare (e.g., *The Seafarers*) to air combat (*The Epic of Flight*), the various tomes were great summations of major historical events. More relevant to this discussion, every one of the volumes was chock full of gorgeous artwork (Time-Inc. clearly had a rights acquisition and commissioning budget that rivaled most small nations' GDP). Want to see an artist's representation of what it looked like inside a dreadnought at Jutland? These books had you covered. Wonder what it might have looked like over the Bekaa Valley during Operation Mole Cricket? There's a painting for that. Across the dozens of books, I was introduced to many artists whose names have gradually faded from common knowledge. Thomas Lea took me to the skies above the U.S.S. *Hornet* as she fought for her life off Santa Cruz. John A. Hamilton's images transported me to the North Atlantic as the Royal Navy battled the *Kriegsmarine*. Finally, Fred W. Freeman's drawings brought life (and death) aboard U.S. destroyers and submarines during World War II to the vivid fore. All these works were an oasis of the soul for a young budding historian spending his summers stuck in rural Missouri.

Fast forward several decades to the start of my own independent author career. I was certain of the need for similarly magnificent images for my books, and thankfully, I was smart enough to marry an artist, Anita C. Young. Throughout her career she has not only won awards, but has also had several excellent instructors who taught her the *why* of art. In her patient, ever loving way (okay, fine, we argued…*a lot*), Anita gradually showed me that there are *reasons* to do art a certain way. More importantly, she explained the *language* of art, allowing me to convey the images in my head into something artists could actually turn into paintings and illustrations. Fellow authors, some of whom were excellent artists as well, served as professional sounding boards (even if we didn't always see eye to eye). With every interaction I gained ideas for images that people would find appealing not just as covers, but also as standalone pieces. Throughout my career thus far, I've observed best practices (i.e., authors are seldom sorry if they get the full rights to their cover art) and lessons in professionalism (i.e., *pay your artists for their work*). The results of this education are found in the following pages.—The Slinger, July 2025

Haynes Makes a Killing

(From *Acts of War*)

Anita C. Young, 2014

Every published author holds a special place for their first cover. The impetus behind this cover was my desire to present a situation that was clearly ahistorical. To achieve this, Anita rendered the *Spitfire* Mark IX in Dutch East Indies colors. The mottled jungle scheme and distinctive orange triangle have served as immediate "cues" to many aviation historians at comic conventions. The more astute have noted that the combat depicted is taking place at high altitude (see cloud base), and that the victim is an Imperial Japanese *Hayabusa* fighter, the ubiquitous "*Oscar*." A great first cover, even if I shortly thereafter found out it doesn't make business sense to have differing e-book and print edition covers. Live and learn, unlike this IJA pilot.

Battle of Hawaii

(From *Acts of War*)

Wayne Scarpaci, 2014

Just as an author remembers their first cover, they also remember the first work they procured from a cherished cover artist. Anita famously declared "I don't do ships…" (keep this in mind) when I presented the concept for this painting. Being a stubborn sort and wanting to bring my vision to life, I set out in search of someone who *did* do ships. Initially I found a KC local comic book artist who specialized in World War II pieces and asked him to do three scenes from the manuscript (i.e., the eponymous "Acts" from the book's title). The end result was fantastic… and convinced everyone who saw it that I was making a gorgeous graphic novel.

Enter Wayne Scarpaci, who I contacted after finding some examples of his art via a Google search. Initially my plan was to use some of his already completed art for *Acts of War*'s print cover. For various reasons (namely some author mentors clubbing me about the head and shoulders), I quickly realized that a unique, custom cover would do much better. As with the "Haynes Makes a Killing," I wanted to have something that was an immediate, "That is ***wrong***…" from the plot. Well, you don't get much more wrong than the *Arizona* underway while under attack from the *Kido Butai*'s carrier air group. This is one of my most popular collaborations, so much so that it's "earned out" in print sales since I started doing conventions.

Collisions of the Damned

(From *Collisions of the Damned*)

Anita C. Young (2015)

Historically, the Japanese invasion of the Dutch East Indies is known as the first time the Imperial Japanese Navy (IJN) demonstrated its night fighting prowess during World War II. As *Acts of War* and *Collisions of the Damned* were originally just one novel (hmm, wonder how big that book would have been… oh, wait), it didn't occur to me to have a cover that paid homage to that fact. But once I split the two books, it seemed appropriate for the second book's cover to reflect this event.

Remember Anita's claim that she "didn't do ships" under the last entry? Well, as you can see, she was clearly underestimating her own abilities. Historically, the only British battleship lost during this phase of the Pacific War was the unlucky *Prince of Wales,* along with the battlecruiser *Repulse*. So, the ahistorical trigger in this one is a clearly British BB (whose name I won't share for spoilers' sake) sinking while under the light of star shells. Despite this, you would be *shocked* at the number of people who ask me, "Is that *Barham?*" It just goes to show that a grand old lady can have one of the most oft-broadcast demises in history and the details (i.e., daylight, capsizes the opposite direction, ship class) are easily misremembered. Honestly, I think the only other contender for most repeated demise might be *Arizona*. *Barham*'s demise, however, being easy to obtain and license, has been used in multiple films and television shows, whereas *Arizona* is usually only seen in documentaries. Alas, this work isn't often seen due to the dark colors just not printing all that well.

Death of *Kongo*

(From *On Seas So Crimson*)

Wayne Scarpaci (2014)

Here is a fact that might surprise you: The four *Kongo*-class battleships never operated as a complete division during World War II. As the class were originally constructed as battlecruisers, they were the only battleships capable of keeping up with the *Kido Butai* to ensure Nagumo's Finest First Air Fleet didn't get the *Glorious* treatment. Alas, the fact they were also the most fuel efficient and maneuverable Japanese battleships also resulted in their being most often put at risk. I leaned heavily into this in the *Usurper's War* universe, which is how they all found themselves trading blows with Allied capital ships in the Java Sea. Spoiler alert: It doesn't go well for poor *Kongo*, for as you can see here, she's channeling her British design roots at the hands of one of her Royal Navy "cousins."

Originally this piece was going to be the hard copy cover for *Collisions of the Damned*. However, as discussed with the two pieces from *Acts of War*, it became readily apparent that this was rather dumb as it confuses customers. Simultaneously, due to some corporate acquisitions and reorganization, it became cheaper to combine the first two *Usurper's War* novels into one collection (*On Seas So Crimson*), rather than print them separately. This also conveniently allowed me to technically carry more books to cons / wheel and deal with specials. I was happy to use this work as the dual-story cover. It was only after much "art critique" from Anita, backed up by several con fans, that I became aware people confused "The Battle of Hawaii" and this piece. Yes, hard core grognards could point out that *Arizona* and *Kongo* look nothing alike, but the average layman goes "Big gray ship on fire…" This was a lesson learned when deciding on the next few pieces.

Suffering of the *Suffren*

(From *Against the Tide Imperial*)

Anita C. Young (2019)

There was a rather large gap between *Collisions of the Damned* and *Against the Tide Imperial*. The break was both planned (I had a Ph.D. to finish and sci-fi universe to write another book for) and unplanned (switched day jobs, had a few other life events). This turned out to be a good thing, as when I ("FINALLY"—very vocal fans) got back around to the *Usurper's War* universe, I had several new ideas. First, I'd read quite a few good books on carrier operations, and on the naval aspects of Operation Torch. Second, I realized that there was very little alternative history where the Royal Navy ended up fighting the IJN in the Indian Ocean. Finally, and tangentially related, I discovered that the Imperial Japanese Army (IJA) had a plan to seize Ceylon in early 1942. This in and of itself was not unusual. The IJA seemed to have a plan for invading *everyone* and *everywhere* in the early days of World War II, which basically led to the IJN constantly having to go, "Okay, cool beans, with what sea lift?" Anyone who knows how much the IJA and IJN hated each other can imagine how well *that* went. Combined, this led to the general concept that unfolds in *Against the Tide Imperial*.

Once again, I turned to Anita (you know, the person who can't draw ships) to put my mental vision into action. Unsurprisingly, my mental vision had some serious marketing deficiencies. For instance, in the book, this scene has the American *Dauntlesses* with black tails for easy recognition purposes. Guess what doesn't show up well against the dark blue waters of the Indian Ocean off South Africa? That's right, black tails. Did I go full on "rivet counter" in arguing for the scene's accuracy? Vehemently and stubbornly. Did I eventually have to concede once we ran it past some folks? Also yes. The art lesson learned here? Trust artists. There's a reason most of us authors are not doing our own covers. In my defense, I did listen and make sure the ship involved in this cover was *not* a battleship and that the color scheme was different. The *Suffren* doesn't show up in a lot of alternate history, so that was an additional perk.

AI-154

A Victorious Meeting

(From *Against the Tide Imperial / The Victorious Meeting*)

Itifonhom (2020)

Meeting artists is often about luck. I happened to be scrolling through Facebook when a bunch of World War II aviation artwork came across my feed. Good, crisp digital pictures, several of which involved classic warbirds from the P-51 to the less common Me-210. A little bit of "extrovert powers activate…" added to some lively discussions about aircraft, and I'd hired Itifonhom for "Snakeyes for *Hermes*" (which you'll meet later). However, I was so happy with that piece, I commissioned him for some additional art I intended to use for Facebook and Bookbub adverts.

Although I made sure to file down the narrative's detachment points so they were not as noticeable, folks can probably pick up that *Against the Tide Imperial* had a Royal Navy arc. I have always found it fascinating to try and work out what would happen if the RN and IJN, being former allies, came to blows.

Unfortunately, *Against the Tide Imperial* was already a pretty hefty, wide-ranging book with a large cast of characters. Adding another 10-20,000 words would have made it a true monster, and I knew at some point I'd be doing a climatic, likely larger book 4. As I try to avoid making collections that can double as siege ammunition, it was clear something had to go. Thus when I asked Itifonhom to do this piece, I made sure to specify it had to have space for Anita to make it into a cover. Thus, when I got back around to writing the novella *The Victorious Meeting*, I had cover art ready to go. In addition to a *Seafire* fighting a *George* in *Akagi* markings, the other ahistorical problem is that the British fighter's national insignia would have only been on the fuselage and upper surface of the port wing. In-universe, the national insignia on *both* wings is explained as a way to differentiate from Usurper forces.

Taiho

(From *Against the Tide Imperial*)

Wayne Scarpaci, 2024

Speaking of the cover to the *Usurper's War* Collection #2 (tentatively titled *In Violence So Decisive*), this piece is currently the leading candidate. By this point in our business relationship, I realized I could trust Wayne to do a sweeping piece that fit *Against the Tide Imperial*'s climactic battle scene. For sharp eyed World War II buffs, the ahistorical setting is pretty clear: The *Taiho* died from a single torpedo hit delivered from the submarine U.S.S. *Albacore*. This wound was only fatal because the carrier's damage control officer had a deep, persistent bout of the stupids. In contrast, the *Taiho* is clearly catching the business from multiple torpedo bombers, has an out of control avgas fire, and is not answering her helm on account of "bridge is on fire, please send graves and registration." Given what has happened to the Allies up to this point in *Against the Tide Imperial*, this is a deeply cathartic outcome for the USN.

Thunderbolt and *Lightnings*

(From *Against the Tide Imperial*)

Itifonhom, 2024

Given my subject matter, I'm often asked what my favorite World War II fighter is. My answer is always, "If it's Europe or the Med, the P-47. If I'm the Pacific though, it's the P-38. I don't trust the little old lady at the engine factory that much." It should therefore be little to no surprise that I'd find a way to work *Thunderbolts* and *Lightnings* into the plot of *Against the Tide Imperial*. In this case, it's a risky yet beautifully executed ambush of the *Kido Butai*'s strike against the RN's Eastern Fleet. Itifonhom did a bang-up job both with the lighting and the very ahistorical, Southeast Asia / Burma color scheme against the Indian Ocean. As with several other pieces in this book, the large version on the front of my table never ceases to bring a curious person from dozens of feet away.

BASTOGNE

Tiger Tamers of Bastogne

(From *Hooves, Tracks, and Sabers/Missives From The Green*)

Justin Adams, 2025

Another thing I used to hear A LOT at conventions: "Wait, you're a former tanker?! Why don't you ever do tank combat?!" I say "used to hear," because in 2023 I agreed to do three (later expanded to four) anthologies for a small outfit in Texas called Raconteur Press. For *Hooves, Tracks, and Sabers*, the second anthology, the theme was mounted combat. It has everything from Carthaginian heavy cavalry to World War II armored combat. My contribution had Lieutenant General Leslie McNair come to an untimely end in a plane crash in 1943. While it is *slightly* harsh to hang all of American armor's shortcomings on him, McNair is widely considered to be the man most responsible for the *Sherman* arriving in France with only a 76mm gun. With him quite dead, I posited that not only would the U.S. Army have gotten the T26 (later M26) *Pershing* earlier, but that American ordnance officers, like their British counterparts, would have found some way to do "breech fu" and get a 90mm gun onto the *Sherman* chassis. (Google "Sherman Firefly" and then "Super Sherman" for an example of just what kind of chicanery could be pulled on an M-4's hull).

As with most of my anthologies, Raconteur Press only held the rights to "Blackjack at Bastogne" for one year. I'm highly motivated to maximize profit from the intellectual property and copyrights I control. So with all four stories reverting back to me by November 2025, I set about trying to find an eye-catching cover for this future collection. Unfortunately, I was met with various conflicts of time and space with my usual World War II artists, so I took a flyer and asked Justin Adams if he wanted to give things a shot. For those who are not familiar with his work, Justin is usually a sci-fi and speculative fiction artist. I had a concept, some reference pictures… and not a whole lot else. To say that he knocked it out of the park would be an understatement. Indeed, this piece has been so well received that even though it's not six months old, yet it's already earned out. Is it my favorite? Well, that's like asking a parent who their favorite child is. But did I have a decal of it made for the back of my vehicle? Why yes, yes I did.

"But James, if you planned on it for being the cover for your future collection, why is it the cover for *this* book?" Well, given its performance at Galaxycon Oklahoma City, it became clear to me that something about this piece just draws fans like moths to the flame. A little later, I also realized that mixing alternative history and science fiction probably wasn't going to work, plus I had enough short stories in both to do separate collections. So I decided if people loved it, what better thing to use as the cover of the art book? Plus *Raconteur Days* has now become the short story collections *Missives From the Green* (alternate history) and *Tales From the Confederation* (sci-fi).

Wonder No More

(From *Wonder No More*)

Wayne Scarpaci, 2023

There are many schools of thought on what makes a good cover piece. On one hand, you have folks that believe a cover can convey the general *theme* of a book but doesn't have to necessarily reflect either events or actual characters in the book. I vehemently adhere to the opposite viewpoint, i.e., "If it's on the cover, it happens inside the book." Which has led to some rather interesting outcomes, as often I will have a mental *concept* of a scene but not necessarily figured out the plan for how to get there. This was the case with "Wonder No More," as weird things had happened during the "wargaming phase" of plot development. I am very minimal in my application of plot armor. Indeed, unless it will contradict some other work or previously established timeline, I stand by fluke outcomes, like Type 93 "Long Lances" hitting the U.S.S. *Alabama* at extreme range. War is full of utterly chaotic misfortune, and it is sometimes fun to have to write my way out of things.

The Battle of Leyte Gulf has fascinated me since I was a kid. So much so that I wrote an article defending Vice Admiral William Halsey for *Naval History*'s 80th Anniversary issue, have advocated for Commander Ernest Evans (U.S.S. *Johnston*) to have a destroyer named after him in *Proceedings*, and did a Leyte Gulf episode on the "Mother of Tanks" podcast. In retrospect, it shouldn't be surprising I wrote a novella on the battle, but rather only that it took me this long to do so. Unfortunately given the tactical situation, I was not able to perform "fan service" and have the greatly desired "*Iowa* vs. *Yamato*" throwdown. I think U.S.N. "heavy metal" that's present in this picture, however, is more than enough recompense.

3-A-307
ARMADA
07

Snakeyes for *Hermes*

(From *Dispatches From Valhalla*)

Itifonhom, 2019

The Falklands War was one of my earliest "news" memories as a child. *Newsweek* magazine had extensive coverage of the conflict, and I remember both the famous "The Empire Strikes Back" and extensive hand-wringing coverage after the *Sheffield* caught an *Exocet*. As the years have passed, I've returned to it in multiple ways (e.g., papers, casual history conversations, and even my dissertation). For such a seminal conflict, it is quite surprising how little historical fiction, much less alternate history, has addressed it, but it was always on my, "Hmm, someday I need to do a story…"-list. I finally checked that block in 2019, as "Fate of the Falklands" was my contribution to a nautical alternate history anthology I edited for a small press. My intent was to combine that story, as well as the other two I did for the land and air anthologies, into one collection at some point.

I discussed how Itifonhom and I met back with "The Victorious Meeting." Most of his artwork was World War I and II, so I wanted to make sure he was comfortable doing a modern piece. As there was plenty of time until the story's rights reverted back to me, we had an opportunity for the usual back and forth between artist and client. This was my first big foray into commissioning digital art, and I had no idea about the booming industry of 3-D models out there. The hardest part was, as I recall, finding an accurate model of the *Hermes*. Folks who have seen *Dispatches From Valhalla*, the collection for which this piece eventually became the cover, will note that the *Hermes*' island is on the opposite (i.e., correct) side from the cover. This was due to me being stubborn about some cover "rules," i.e., that cover action should flow from the spine to the book's opening. Live and learn on that one, as in this case the inadvertent ahistorical aspect joined the intentional (e.g., *Skyhawks* never actually hit *Hermes*). Still, even with that snafu, it's nice to have a modern cover to break up the parade of World War II pieces on my table.

Scat X

Robin Takes a Swallow

(From *Violent Blue Yonder*)

Wayne Scarpaci (2024)

In case it isn't clear by this point in the book, Wayne is my usual go-to for nautical pieces. When a man has his artwork in the Nevada Statehouse, has done art for the United States Naval Institute, and received many artistic accolades, you stick with his strengths. Another thing that should be apparent, of course, is that occasionally the opportunity presents itself to ask someone to step out of their comfort zone. Also, as I've gotten "older and wiser" as an indie author, I'm trying to keep the same cover artist for entire series to help with marketing. Enter my *Arc of Ares* series. For various reasons and after some conversations, I opted to "get the band back together" plus add some new folks for another trio of air, land, and sea alternate history anthologies. One of the regrets from the first series was not being able to use some of the scenes from really good stories as cover art.

For instance, Dragon Award Nominee Justin Watson's trio of stories involved an alternate French-Indochina conflict that saw the United States supporting Ho Chi Minh's quest for independence against a Vichy French government. His air story centered on the famous fighter ace Robin Olds, some former American Volunteer Group (a.k.a., "Flying Tigers") pilots, and featured a strong showing of Tuskegee Airmen. (If you recognize Justin's name, it's likely because he's the coauthor of *The Romanov Rescue* along with Kacey Ezell and Tom Kratman.)

If that sounds awesome to you, then you can imagine how badly I wanted to get it painted. Add in an opportunity to have P-80 versus Me-262 *Schwabe* (the eponymous "Swallow"), and the ahistorical setting was easy peasy. I knew Wayne could do ships, but inexplicably (I mean, it's on his website) had not realized he also did aerial art. Once again, brilliant work converting author vision to canvas.

Doty Has a Ball

(From *Dispatches From Valhalla / Thin Red Tales*)

Wayne Scarpaci (2024)

The following is one of my extremely rare violations of the "What's on the tin is what's in the contents…"-rule. If you've read *Thin Red Tales* and are going, "Uh, has he suffered a brain injury? There's totally an M-18 *Hellcat* on North Korean T-34/85 violence in his story…" you're not wrong. However, if you ever see the original of this piece, you'll note that the titular *Hellcat* is *Doty III*. *Doty III* does not make an appearance in "Mr. Dewey's Fire Brigade," my short story in *Thin Red Tales*. Originally my intent was to have the short story "Mr. Dewey's Tank Corps" be my contribution, but then that story went into *Dispatches From Valhalla*. I still toyed with having it in both collections (don't judge me), but then *Dispatches* got picked up for an audiobook. Since I also intended to get *Thin Red Tales* turned into an audiobook at some point, I went ahead and developed a follow up story for M-18 *Hellcats* in Korea. That's right, cover art drove the story for once.

As I'd discovered with our last collaboration, Wayne had drawn several airplanes, but he hadn't done a ton of armor. You would not be able to tell that from the end result, even if I expected a bit much out of an 18 x 24 canvas. Yet even with the scale making the T-34/85 really small, keen-eyed viewers can still identify it. When displayed, it's very amusing watching people immediately recognize the *Hellcat*, try to figure out the target, then have a moment of, "Wait, why are those two vehicles fighting near rice paddies?" My usual response is "Because President Dewey decided Lieutenant Colonel Smith deserved some armor, that's why." This is usually followed by a great conversation, if the person is a Korean war buff and / or served some time in the Land of the Morning Calm.

Wayne

A Stricken Princess

(From *On The Sea*)

Wayne Scarpaci (2024)

The third and final *Arc of Ares* work returned to Wayne's strong suit, the sea. As with "Robin Takes a Swallow," the cover art comprised a selection from another author's short story. Philip's prior contributions in *Violent Blue Yonder* and *Thin Red Tales* involved a timeline where Rome never fell, both of which would have made fine cover art in their own right. However, as you can see, I had plans for both of those anthologies, unlike *On The Sea*. Once we agreed to include "Beatty's Folly," I immediately decided that would be inspiration for the final anthology's cover. I had previously edited the story in 2019 and had, once again, thought it should be the cover for the anthology it was included in. Alas, that anthology publisher chose to go in another direction. One that led to the most common question at cons being, "How is that sailing vessel shooting high explosives into the side of a steel hulled ship?" instead of asking about the stories in the book. As you can tell from this and the last two images, this was a "lesson learned" versus a "lesson observed" when it came time for *Arc of Ares*.

Ironically my strong, fond memories of "Beatty's Folly" led to a moderate mistake on my part. When I talked to Wayne about the picture's concept, I stated it would involve the battlecruiser H.M.S. *Lion* surrendering to the U.S.S. *Georgia*, a "Tillman Battleship." Named for Senator Benjamin Tillman, these behemoths were design concepts that the United States Senate forced the Navy to undertake in the lead up to World War I. Historically, the United States alignment with Great Britain and the blockade of the German High Seas Fleet made the expenditures necessary to field 60-80,000-ton leviathans rather superfluous. Philip set the table to bring these monsters to life… and also had the *Lion* come to an end that would have made this painting impossible. There went the idea of titling this work "Teddy's *Lion* Tamer," but thankfully Beatty's flagship had a sister that the story never directly dealt with "on screen." Enter the H.M.S. *Princess Royal*, forced to strike her colors to an opposing capital ship that was a third larger and more than double her displacement. The only hiccup was figuring out which of the Tillman designs to go with, but a little historical research allowed Wayne and I to choose an imposing, yet historically realistic design.

Real amusement, of course, would be writing a timeline where the modernized Tillmans end up facing off with the *Yam*… nope, nope, not speaking that into existence. The most important thing an author can do is figure out when to stop the good idea train. Much like the *Princess Royal*'s captain, a wise person knows when it's time to fold.

About the Artists

Artist Bio: Justin Adams

Justin Adams is a New York City-based illustrator and concept artist whose story-driven visuals have become a hallmark across film, gaming, and publishing. With over a decade of experience, Adams blends classical technique with modern digital fluency to create compelling imagery that resonates on both a narrative and emotional level.

His work spans diverse genres—sci-fi, fantasy, horror—and is particularly noted for its thoughtful use of composition, color, and symbolism. Whether crafting concept art as the foundation of visual storytelling or standalone illustrations that function as complete narrative vessels, Justin excels in building immersive worlds. He has illustrated covers for numerous novels and genre publications such as *Apex Magazine* and worked on game titles for EA Sports and Upper Deck Entertainment. Alongside his commercial work, he is a dedicated mentor, sharing his craft through the artist collective *The Anvil*, where he believes "when you teach, you learn twice."

Where You Can Find Justin

https://justinadams77.crevado.com/justin-adams

Artist Bio: Itifonhom

Anastasios Polychronis is a digital aviation artist. Born in1971 and based near Frankfurt am Main, Germany, he started creating digital aviation art in 2010. He has contributed illustrations for many publications since then, including magazines, books, and scale model box art. His client list includes Osprey Publishing, Kagero, Britain at War Magazine, Flugzeug Classic Magazine, RS models, Roden and many more publications. Itifonhom studied graphic design in Thessaloniki, Greece.

Where you can find Itifonhom

www.itifonhom.com

Artist Bio: Wayne Scarpaci

Wayne was born into a career Navy family in 1950. He grew upon and around naval ships and naval stations. At five years old he began drawing the ships he so frequently saw. In his teens he was a U.S. Naval Sea Cadet and was aboard many types of vessels. In 1966 he enlisted in the Army's *Nike* Missile Program and was stationed at an Air Defense Command Post in Germany. After discharge, Wayne worked as a computer field service engineer on many military and civilian projects. He also served with the California Army Guard on 8" self-propelled field artillery.

His art skills are entirely self-taught. Wayne has art on display aboard many museum ships, in the Nevada statehouse, in international naval museums, and the United States Naval Academy in Annapolis, Maryland. Wayne is also an accomplished author as well as an award-winning artist. His published book bibliography currently includes seven battleship technical reference titles, a technical title on a railroad, and a work on fitness and nutrition over 60. He currently resides in Nevada.

Where You Can Find Wayne

www.artbywayne.net

Artist Bio: Anita C. Young

Anita C. Young is the winner of the 2018 Pollack Purchase Award from Washburn University, and winner of Best in Show for the Human Experience versus Abstract Exhibition at the Tomahawk Art Center. Her passion is to create artworks that focus on mental health to make open dialogue easier. She is now a full-time freelance artist and focuses primarily on pet portraits. Choosing to create pet portraits was a natural outcrop of mental health given all the benefits, mental and physical, our pets give us. When she has free time, she is also a writer. She has written one complete urban fantasy series and is currently working on her young adult fantasy series.
Anita C. Young was born and raised in Canada before marrying a U.S. Army officer. The couple moved around the world before finally settling in Topeka, KS, where she obtained her B.S. in Medical Laboratory Science from Washburn in 2010. After almost a decade of serving the community at a local hospital, Ms. Young decided to pursue her lifetime love of art at Washburn.

Where You Can Find Anita:

Username @anitacyoung on the following social media platforms—

www.anitacyoung.com

The Bio of the Guy Who Hired All Those Fine Artists

James Young is an American author of science fiction, alternative history, and post-apocalyptic fiction. His primary series is the *Usurper's War*, which is set in an alternate history where Adolf Hitler is killed by an RAF bomb in November 1940. He is also the author of *The Vergassy Chronicles*, a military sci-fi universe set in the 3050s. In addition to his own work, James has edited anthologies including bestselling authors Sarah Hoyt, S.M. Stirling, and David Weber. His non-fiction writing credits include *Eagles, Ravens, and Other Birds of Prey*, winning the United States Naval Institute's (USNI's) 2016 Cyberwarfare Essay Contest, and various articles in *Armor*, *The Journal of Military History*, and *Proceedings*.

Where You Can Find James

www.ingramcontent.com/pod-product-compliance
Lightning Source LLC
Chambersburg PA
CBHW041637050726
47507CB00026B/198
9781963830118